21 Cousins

By Diane de Anda

Illustrated by Isabel Muñoz

STAR BRIGHT BOOKS

CAMBRIDGE MASSACHUSETTS

Hardcover ISBN-13: 978-1-59572-915-6
Paperback ISBN-13: 978-1-59572-916-3
Star Bright Books / MA / 00104210
Printed in China / Toppan / 9 8 7 6 5 4 3 2 1

Printed on paper from sustainable forests.

Library of Congress Cataloging-in-Publication Data

Names: De Anda, Diane, author. Muñoz, Isabel, illustrator.
Title: 21 cousins / by Diane de Anda ; illustrated by Isabel Muñoz.
Other titles: Twenty-one cousins
Description: Cambridge, Massachusetts : Star Bright Books, [2021]
   Audience: Ages 4-8. Audience: Grades K-1. Summary: Siblings
   Alejandro and Sofia celebrate their rich Latinx and mestizo heritage, as
   well as the traits that make each of their cousins unique, when they
   gather for a special family reunion. Spanish words and their meanings
   are interspersed in the text.
Identifiers: LCCN 2020046299 ISBN 9781595729156 (hardcover) ISBN
   9781595729163 (paperback) ISBN 9781595729231 (paperback)
Subjects: CYAC: Cousins--Fiction. Family reunions--Fiction. Latin
   Americans--Fiction. Mestizos--Fiction. Racially mixed
   people--Fiction.
Classification: LCC PZ7.D3474 Aah 2021 DDC [E]--dc23
LC record available at https://lccn.loc.gov/2020046299

Rosa María y Juanita '55

Abuelo Pedro y Abuela María 1953

Abuelo Juan y Abuela Marta

This is our family photo album, filled with the faces of grandparents, parents, aunts, uncles, and 21 cousins. Our mom and dad each have a brother and two sisters, and they have children too. This makes us all cousins.

We call ourselves *familia* because we are a Latino family. A first cousin in Latino families is called a *primo hermano* or *prima hermana*, which means a special kind of brother or sister.

Recuerdo de tío Roberto

Tío Agustín

Tía Paula 1988

Our family is *mestizo*, which means that we share a mixture of the different people and cultures in Mexico: Indian, Spanish, French, and others. This is the reason people in our family look different in many ways. But we are still one family, our *familia*. Come meet our cousins, our *primos* and *primas*.

This is our cousin Enrique. We all call him Kiki. He has long, strong legs and wants to run in the Olympics. He shaves his head to keep cool when he runs.

We call our cousin Elena, *Güera*, because she has honey-colored hair and cream-colored skin that turns golden in the summer sun. She can read and write in English and Spanish and wants to teach in both languages when she grows up.

Tony and his sister, Tonia, have dark brown hair in tight curls. Tony keeps his short because it's easier to take care of on the soccer field. He is almost six feet tall and has a broad chest and big, round arms from lifting weights.

Tonia is tall too and likes to play basketball. She can shoot a basket from across the court. She wears her hair in a curly ponytail on the court.

Teresa has straight, shiny black hair that bounces when she jumps rope. She sings Spanish and English skip-rope rhymes as she jumps. Teresa is a *morena*, which means she has milk-chocolate skin. She looks pretty in her turquoise dress. It makes her brown skin glow.

There are two babies in the family. Miguel is bald. He gives us a big toothless grin when we joke and call him *Pelón* (which means baldy). Ricky has black silky hair and one tooth. Both babies have round, teddy bear bodies. They will probably be best friends when they are older.

Marta and Connie are both in high school. They draw their eyebrows in beautiful arcs above their eyes. Marta's black hair is short and spikey.

Connie lets her long, dark hair fall down her back. She draws dark lines around her almond-shaped eyes. She says she looks like an Aztec princess.

Beto is 8 and goes to a special class in school. He has Down syndrome. Sometimes he needs our help to do things. Most of the time we have fun playing games and sharing our favorite flavor of ice cream, *dulce de leche*, together.

Rudy and Rafael look almost the same because they are twins. Sometimes one is a little taller. Then the other catches up and gets taller. They're both good baseball players. Rudy is a pitcher and Rafael is a shortstop.

Martina is small for her age. My mom says she is petite. We call her Teenie. She does gymnastics and can do a lot of tricks on the bars. When she jumps down from the bars, all the family stands up and claps really loud.

María is the oldest of all the cousins. She looks all grown up and wears her reddish brown hair in a twist at the top of her head, because it's quick and easy. She doesn't have time to fuss with her hair now that she is in college.

Gonzalo is the biggest of all the younger cousins. He is 11 and used to weigh over 150 pounds. He has lost a lot of weight from exercise and a special diet from his doctor so he won't get a sickness called diabetes. We eat fruit together for dessert.

Ruben is 15 and has long hair like everyone else in his band. His hair is really wavy and falls around his face in ringlets that look like little springs. When he plays his drums and shakes his head to the music, all the little springs bounce up and down.

Catalina's nickname is *Chata* because she has a cute, little button nose. She has green eyes and light brown hair, which she likes to wear in French braids. She wants to be a dancer. She is only 8, but can do hip-hop, salsa, ballet, and dance with castanets.

Mario is 17 and fixes all the computers in the family. He and his friends play games on the computer, especially ones with wizards, dragons, and other creatures. They usually wear black clothes. Mario shaves the sides of his head, but gels the top so it stands straight up.

Maricela is very smart. She can spell words in Spanish and English. This year, she won the third-grade spelling bee. We all cheered when she rolled up the ramp to get her trophy. Her picture was in the newspaper, smiling with her sleek black hair in two ponytails and happy brown eyes.

I'm Alejandro and I have hair and eyes the color of root beer. I comb my hair to the side, but it hangs straight down when I'm upside down on the monkey bars. My cousins call me *Payaso*, which means clown because I'm always doing things to make people laugh.

I'm Sofía and my brown eyes have little specks of green. In the fall and winter, I spend a lot of time indoors, so my face looks lighter and my hair darker. In the spring and summer, I'm in the sun all day with the junior swim team. My hair becomes lighter and my skin turns a caramel color. So, even by myself, I can look different ways and still be me.

All 21 cousins are here today to welcome cousin number 22, Baby Cristina! We are glad that all 21 cousins are the same and different in many ways. But most of all, we're glad to be the same in one way: we're family, our *familia*.